MOONLIGHT DESIRES

A CINDERELLA RETELLING

DAVID TOCHER

DAVID TOCHER

RAVE REVIEWS

"David Tocher is a Wizard of Words and a Master of Literary Mayhem...and in addition to being a superb writer, he is also a very nice and very cool guy. I highly recommend David and his work!"
—Stephen Spignesi, New York Times-bestselling author of *Stephen King, American Master*

"One of the true Masters of the Macabre, David Tocher is a rare writer who goes beyond genre. He invites you into his worlds and makes you forget the one you live in. David's writing changes everything."
—Daniela Acitelli, Audiobook Narrator and YouTube Host

"Tocher's writing hits hard and fast, then lingers … His prose carries the rhythm of folklore but is sharp with modern sensibility."
—Thomas Anderson, Editor-in-Chief, *Literary Titan*

"Tocher revels in body horror … The horror is fresh, unsettling, and deeply personal."
—Neena H. Brar for *The Prairies Book Review*

"When you read a David Tocher story, the fat is trimmed and you're left with a raw, solid tale of unique storytelling that leaves you entertained and wanting seconds."
—Anthony Northrup, author of the *Stephen King Dollar Baby* series

"David Tocher is a new voice with a dedicated desire to reveal to us the haunting spaces between worlds."

DAVID TOCHER

— Nancy Kilpatrick, author of *Thrones of Blood* series

"David Tocher is a master storyteller whose imagination knows no equal. His stories transport you into realms that will make you never want to return to reality."
— Karen Dales, author of *The Chosen Chronicles*

"I could read Tocher all day long, rain or shine. You can tell when a writer has immersed himself in the literary greats. Tocher is such a talent."
— James Pyne, author of *FUEL*

"David Tocher is not only a great writer, he's also a master craftsman in the art of storytelling."
— Franklin E. Wales, author of *The Legacy of Frankenstein*

MOONLIGHT DESIRES

This tale is dedicated to Samantha Chambers
and Anthony Northrup,
wonderful friends and colleagues.
And a special hello to Gena!

DAVID TOCHER

CONTENTS

Author's Preface

The following story was found handwritten in the journal of Charlotte Sophia Janicker (1835–1902). In another of her journals, she recounts disturbing dreams in which she saw singular, dissociated events that lingered in her mind long after she awoke. They lingered, she explained, because they felt real, as though someone else's memories were passing through her.

Unable to silence these visions, she resolved to shape them into stories. As she wrote, "There is no better way to contrive a story to hang these visions on than to take one that already exists and refashion it accordingly." And so, Charlotte chose *Cinderella*.

Some passages of her tale were missing; the pages were either lost, or the ink was faded. Where needed, I filled in these gaps, doing my best to preserve her voice. To do so, I read as many versions of Cinderella from different cultures as I could, borrowing the details that best completed her fragments.

At times I copied the Brothers Grimm directly to bridge sections of narrative; at other moments I wrote the lines myself, drawing inspiration from Yeh-Shen, the Chinese Cinderella, or from other cultural variations. In this way, the story you now hold is a collaborative effort across time.

Another classical narrative Charlotte drew from was the story of Arachne in Ovid's *Metamorphoses* (Book VI, Fable I). She took many liberties with it, recasting Minerva as a lady of noble birth and Arachne as an unnamed peasant woman. In Charlotte's retelling, the roles are reversed: it is the peasant who curses the princess (who serves as the mortal stand-in for the goddess).

You may find the ending somewhat abrupt. That is because Charlotte herself concluded her retelling in this way. My writer's instinct urged me to extend it—to fashion an ending more satisfying for the reader—but I refrained, wishing to remain as faithful to Charlotte's original work as possible.

Another puzzle I encountered was the "Ingridelite Weave," which Charlotte references throughout this tale. I proposed to Karen and Amelia Janicker, who commissioned this project, that I fill in the gaps by imaginatively inventing my own illustration and explanation of this element's purpose. They refused, insisting the story be left as is. When I pressed them for any knowledge they might have of the Ingridelite Weave, they both declined to speak.

Finally, I am honoured that Karen Janicker (who told me to just call her "Mama Kay") and her granddaughter, Amelia, entrusted me with this task. I also wish to thank Madison Perth, who first referred them to me. Maddy and I go way back. I remember when we were both starting out as writers, hustling to sell books at conventions. She went on to become an internationally known bestselling author, while I have kept a modest but loyal following among horror readers. Indeed, her and I live in different literary worlds, yet we have never failed to be there for one another. You're the best, Maddy!

So, without further ado, I hope you enjoy Moonlight Desires.

—*Dave Tocher*
October 5th, 2025
West Kelowna, British Columbia

DAVID TOCHER

"The effect of the full moon in such a state of brilliancy was manifold. It acted on dreams, it acted on lunacy, it acted on nervous people, it had marvelous physical influences connected with life."

—Sheridan Le Fanu, *Carmilla*

"How swift, how swift from left and right
The racing fields and hills recede;
Bourns, bridges, rocks, that cross their flight,
In thunders echo to their speed.
'Fear'st thou, my love? the moon shines clear;
Hurrah! how swiftly speed the dead!
The dead does Leonora fear?'
'Ah, no; but talk not of the dead.'"

—Gottfried August Bürger, *Lenore*,
translated by William Robert Spencer

<u>MOONLIGHT DESIRES</u>
"A Cinderella Retelling"

by David Tocher

<u>Part One</u>
Moonlight Desires

Chapter 1

Situated in south-western Ingridel, the region of Shechem was home to a man named Oswald. He was a skilled carpenter and prospered in his work, for many of the nobles of the land sought his craft. Oswald had a daughter named Aurelia, who was beautiful to behold.

Oswald's wife, the mother of Aurelia, taught her how to manage the household and keep the books for the business. But when Aurelia was ten, her mother fell ill. Before she died, she said to Aurelia, "No matter what this world does to you, promise me you'll always stay kind in your heart and in your deeds, even when nothing makes sense."

Then her mother taught her a simple poem, and it was one known only to her and Aurelia:

Toward others, always seek goodwill,
Even if they've done you ill;
All life's trials you may outlive,
If only you learn to forgive.

When Oswald and Aurelia buried her in the cemetery only miles from their home in the countryside, all who knew her mourned, for she was loved and well-favoured throughout the town.

In time Oswald took another wife, Julia, who had a daughter named Lysandra. Julia despised Aurelia for the inheritance's sake, knowing that when Oswald died, all his wealth would pass to Aurelia and not Lysandra. So, Julia stirred up her daughter against her. And Oswald, heeding Julia's words, burdened Aurelia with many hardships.

Lysandra mocked and insulted her in secret. Whenever Aurelia, weary of the abuse, told her to stop, Lysandra would burst into tears, claiming Aurelia had struck her. Her mischief carried into their chores as well: when they washed dishes together, Lysandra would drop the very plates Aurelia had just cleaned. This roused Aurelia's anger, and Lysandra would run off crying, insisting Aurelia had broken the dishes out of hatred, wishing to drive her and Julia away.

When the family—if such a name could rightly be given them—gathered at the dinner table, Julia would weep aloud, demanding to know why Oswald never disciplined his unruly child, and why he allowed his new wife and stepdaughter, whom he had vowed to protect, to suffer such cruelty.

Julia insisted that a hateful, disobedient girl ought to labour for her food. At last, Oswald gave way, forcing Aurelia to shoulder endless chores and bookkeeping to "earn her keep." Some nights grew so cruel that she was left to sleep by the fireplace without supper, unable to finish the impossible burdens pressed upon her.

And it came to pass in those days, that Duke Andrew Chilvers proclaimed a two-day feast so that his twenty-three-year-old son might choose a bride from among the daughters of Shechem. Julia rejoiced for her daughter, while Aurelia also longed to go. But she had no dress, knew nothing of dancing, and the household laughed at her for daring to dream she could attend such a gathering.

Oswald said, "If you clean my shop of every fleck of sawdust, and if you can find yourself a dress and slippers, you may attend." Yet he spoke only to make the task harder, having no intention of letting her go.

So, that evening, Aurelia went to her mother's grave, as she often did, laid flowers there and wept.

A voice asked, "Why do you weep, child?"

Startled, Aurelia gasped and turned her head every which way to find the source of the voice, but she could see no one. She also felt a stab of resentment.

I'm no child! I'm nineteen!

"Who's there?" she asked.

"I am Princess Kipira," came the authoritative reply.

"Princess Kipira?"

"The one and only."

"Well, if you truly are the princess, then please, oh please, do not hide. Show yourself, if you are willing, my liege."

"Are you certain? I am not pleasant to behold now, and humans have come to fear my presence."

"Your Highness, both my father and mother wept when you went missing. I was but a little girl then, and I still remember their loyalty to the crown, which they instilled in me. So please, do not think I will fear you."

"As you wish," Kipira said.

From behind a crooked tombstone, a monstrous black spider emerged, its long, segmented legs creeping through the grass. Rows of shiny, dark-pearl eyes bulged from its furry head.

"So the legend is true!" Aurelia said, looking carefully into those eyes and seeing the honesty of the princess's soul mirrored within.

"Unfortunately, yes."

"Your Highness, if it is not too forward to ask, may I know what caused you to become a spider? I have heard all sorts of strange rumours—oh, wait! Oh! I'm so sorry! Forgive me. Where are my manners?"

Aurelia rose and offered a curtsy, the one every Ingridelite woman was taught to give before a sovereign: extending her right hand, she curled her index and middle fingers, pressed them to her left breast, and curtseyed gracefully (men observed the same finger-to-heart gesture, though with a bow instead).

"Well, Your Highness," she said with a smile, "it will take more than your spidery appearance to frighten me. My name is Aurelia. How may I serve you, my liege?"

"It is I who wish to serve you."

"Whatever do you mean?"

"First, tell me what your mother taught you about kindness, and explain why it is so difficult for you to be kind right now."

Beginning with her mother's passing and continuing through her father and stepmother's conditional offer of letting her attend the festival, Aurelia recounted everything to Princess Kipira, holding nothing back.

Aurelia concluded by saying, "My dear mother told me that kindness isn't only what you do. It is also the intent of your heart. She said I should always seek goodwill toward others, even when someone has hurt me, and the way to do that is through forgiveness. She warned that if someone persists in causing me pain, then—if it is possible—I should distance myself from them, yet still...keep my heart kind toward them.

"But right now, I cannot distance myself from Julia, Lysandra, or even my poor father, whom they have bewitched and turned against me. And though I hold back from saying or doing anything cruel...oh, the bitter thoughts and feelings that surge through me!"

Kipira said, "I don't believe you ought to waste pity on your father. Julia and her sly daughter could not have turned him against you unless some part of him already wished to be turned."

Aurelia's face wore an expression of shock.

"You truly are tender-hearted. The purity of your own heart prevents you from seeing the depravity of others."

"My liege, it feels as though you have dashed to pieces my hope of ever winning my father back."

"This world is cruel, Aurelia," Kipira said softly. "Grief can sour even the noblest of hearts. Perhaps your father cannot endure how much you remind him of his departed wife, and in driving you away, he finds the only comfort left to him."

Aurelia's eyes filled with tears again, and she struggled to contain them. "He wishes to...disown and forget me forever...and start over with a new family."

"The tender mercies of the wicked are cruel," Princess Kipira said. "But be of good courage, Aurelia. You have nothing to fear. What you have lost will not be the best you will ever have.

I will see to it that you attend the festival tonight."

"But how? My father and Julia have already taken Lysandra. There is no other horse or carriage for me. My only chance is tomorrow, if I can finish my chores."

"I will provide the dress, the carriage, the horse, and the coachmen—and they will be unlike anything you have seen before. You will make it tonight, but only if you obey me carefully."

Hope returned to Aurelia's face. "Oh yes, Your Highness! I will follow every word."

"Then we must not lose another moment," said Kipira, leading her beyond the cemetery gates into a clearing. The princess spun a vast web and spread it like a silken carpet across the grass.

"Sit upon my web. I will carry you home."

"But how can you know the way if I haven't—"

"I am a spider. I silently watch everything and everyone from the webs I weave. I know where you live. Now climb on."

Obediently, Aurelia sat on the thick, gleaming strands.

"Hold fast."

She gripped the silk.

"I trust you're not afraid of speed."

"Oh no, my lady. I love to go fast—the faster, the better."

The princess's eight long legs struck the earth, and the web, tethered to her spinnerets, skimmed just above the ground. Wind rushed past, whipping Aurelia's golden hair behind her.

"Oh, faster, please, Your Highness—if you are willing."

"I held back, fearing to frighten you. But I can go faster still."

"Yes, please!"

Kipira quickened her stride. The world blurred past. Trees, rocks, farmhouses flashing into streaks of colour. Aurelia's dress rippled against her skin. Her hair streamed wildly in the wind, and she laughed with unrestrained delight. For the first time in years, her sorrow fell away, replaced by a soaring joy.

nside her father's shop, Aurelia watched with wonder as Princess Kipira used that same silken carpet, dragging it throughout the entire space. Every piece of sawdust stuck to the web until the shop was entirely clean.

"Now, your chores are complete," said Kipira. "There is nothing your father or your stepmother can hold against you."

"Please, if I may ask, why are you doing all of this for me?"

"I will answer that another time. I promise. First, I must weave your dress. And in the meantime, you need to bathe and prepare yourself."

Aurelia obeyed as she had promised. She ran down to a nearby stream, and in a secluded spot, where the stream ran past a large rock and a stand of trees, she was able to bathe in privacy.

When she returned, the sun had set, and the moonlight was growing.

On the porch hung a dress, woven from Kipira's webs, held up by thin, glimmering strands. It was bathed in moonlight and glowed. Aurelia could hardly believe her eyes. She covered her mouth with her hand and stared at every detail of the delicate garment.

"What are those patterns? Is that...what I think it is?" she whispered.

Kipira's voice was calm but proud. "Yes, dear. This is the Ingridelite Weave. Each part of the pattern is connected to all the rest, so that everything is in everything, even though each part is its own. It is the hardest weave to make in all the land. Some say that only the Royal House of Ingridel knows how to do it."

Aurelia stood quietly, tracing the way each shape fit into the next.

"We can't stay here all night," said Kipira. "We have to get you to the festival."

Aurelia nodded. "Yes, of course. Please help me put it on."

Soon, she was looking at her reflection in the house's front window. The threads of the spider-silk gown clung delicately to her like a second skin. Every strand seemed carefully placed, and she felt like a princess herself.

Then Aurelia noticed that as she moved, the patterns of the Ingridelite Weave shifted with her, the strands locked into a living machinery of dance.

Like someone atop a hill watching a town below, observing its citizens navigate the winding streets, so too did her eyes follow the threads as they slid fluidly through intricate circuits. No design returned to the same place, no motion repeated; each was entirely new. She felt that if she did not guard her attention, she could watch them forever, lost and hypnotized.

As Kipira held up two gossamer slippers with one of her front legs, she said, "Put these on."

Aurelia obeyed. They fit perfectly, and felt firm, yet of silky cotton.

"Now dance, Aurelia," Kipira said.

"But I don't know how."

"What did I tell you in the cemetery about obeying my every word?"

Her cheeks warmed with shame. She apologized, then began moving awkwardly about the porch. Soon the dress itself seemed to guide her. The webs slid and pressed with her steps, shaping them, and before long she danced her way onto the front yard, moving with skill and grace among the moonbeams. She was laughing aloud with joy.

"The moonlight works on the webs and fills them with a strange vitality," said Kipira. "Don't ask me how. It just does."

"Whatever the moon is doing, it is wonderful!"

She danced a while longer until Kipira said she must be off to the festival.

The princess's fanged appendages grated together, their bristled hairs rasping into a low, retching cry. The noise made Aurelia's stomach twist. She clutched her ears and stumbled back.

From the darkness emerged a stagecoach, four horses, and a coachman, each formed entirely of webs. Moonlight glimmered on them as the horses tossed their heads and whinnied, moving with a lifelike grace. Yet the wheels and hooves made no sound upon the earth.

The coachman shouted a sharp "Hi-yah!" and the horses surged forward, galloping faster.

She understood. That awful sound had been a summons.

Aurelia cried out with delight and begged to touch them. Kipira raised a foreleg, the nearest gesture to a nod of assent she could give. Aurelia reached out, and the horses nuzzled against her. Their manes were soft under her fingers, yet their bodies were hollow and thin as mist.

"My webs come alive in the lesser light that rules the night," said Kipira. "Yet no matter how dazzling or intricately woven they may be, they are hollow, empty, and they dissolve into nothing at dawn, when they are exposed to the greater light that rules the day, and the Desires that inhabit them return to the underworld."

"What do you mean by 'Desires'?" asked Aurelia.

"To desire is to long for something absent. The underworld is indeed a place of absence—of love, of light, of fellowship. And thus the spirits from that place who inhabit my woven forms are defined by their primary quality: their longing. These spirits of the underworld are called Desires, and these, indeed, are Moonlight Desires."

"There was a time," she continued, her voice catching, "when I was so lonely I made such creatures each night—different shapes, different faces—to speak with me, to befriend me. And every morning I wept as they dissolved into nothing beneath the rising sun. It was a bitter reminder of my curse, of my isolation.

"For that reason I ceased making them long ago. But for you, Aurelia, on this very night, I have made an exception."

Aurelia understood, but sorrow touched her heart all the same.

"As long as you wear the slippers, the coachman will obey you," said Princess Kipira. "Be sure to return home before dawn, for I have already warned you what sunrise will do. And remember this…speak your name to no man while you wear the dress at night, nor let any man discover your name, for if you do, all will vanish as though touched by the sun. Don't ask why because I do not know. The power that binds me is strange and riddled with anomalies."

Aurelia smiled and said, "You're a strange animal, that's what I know."

"Duke Andrew is a good man, loyal to my mother and father, and I can think of no better match for his son than you. If you marry him, you will join my nobility, and we will see each other again when I return to human form. Now go!"

The door to the stagecoach opened, and webbed stairs unfolded beneath it. In awe, Aurelia climbed them, then settled into her seat within. Its webs conformed perfectly to her body, and there was a bit of a bounce. The steps folded back up and the door closed behind her.

"Where to, m'lady?" asked the coachman, turning to look at her.

"To the castle of Duke Andrew."

"Yes, m'lady," he replied, and with a crack of his whip and another sharp "Hi-yah!" the horses began their silent gallop across the ground.

Aurelia felt as though she were sitting in a strange boat that was rising and falling with the waves of a strange sea.

"Sir?" said Aurelia.

"Yes, m'lady?"

"I like to go fast. Can you go fast for me?"

The coachman turned his hollow, webbed head to look at her again. He was grinning, and Aurelia's stomach sank when she saw the emptiness of the eyes and the mouth. They seemed like portals into a living darkness, where things existed that she did not want to imagine.

"There is a saying, m' lady. It goes *'Denn die Todten reiten schnell.'* Do you know what that means?"

"I do not, sir."

He grinned again, the corners of his mouth stretching up to his ears, revealing double rows of pointed teeth, made of webs. Aurelia's blood ran cold at the sight.

"Oh, you better hold on tight, dearie, because it means the Dead travel fast!"

And with that, he turned himself around and urged the horses to gallop faster.

She gripped the webbed walls of the stagecoach and held on as tight as she could, digging her feet into the floor's sticky strands. The webs stretched and enveloped them but did not break. Then, as the horses quickened their pace along the dirt trail through the forest, their strides grew faster and faster, until Aurelia felt as though she were flying.

Past the evergreens they raced, over the trail—sometimes straight, sometimes winding—beneath an arch of moonlight and a sky spangled with stars. Whenever the coach veered sharply left or right, Aurelia's body pitched the other way, flung sideways by the turn. Looking up through the translucent roof, she saw how the stars seemed to streak across the heavens like celestial lifeblood coursing through arteries of light.

With the air blowing back her hair and causing the webs of her dress to ripple against her body, Aurelia held on tighter and shouted, "This is *amazing*! I love being alive!"

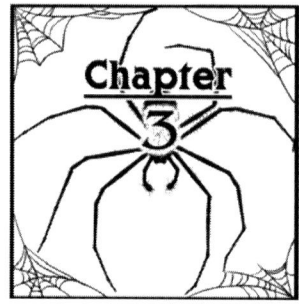

Chapter 3

The narrow cobblestone path wound its way under a high canopy of evergreens until the forest opened in a meadow before a wrought-iron gate. Upon a rocky hill, thickly carpeted with moss, rose Duke Andrew's castle: its stone walls darkened by age, its roofs sharply pitched, as if striving toward the sky. Turrets and towers crowned with spires, and the pointed arches of doors and windows, drew the eye heavenward.

As the gate lowered and Aurelia's silken stagecoach rolled across the threshold, a wave of awe and solitude swept over her. She felt small before this ancient edifice, which had witnessed all that had unfolded within the forest and, in a manner of speaking, had become one with it.

Aurelia soon entered the duke's inner courtyard and saw her father and stepmother attempting to console Lysandra, who could not find a single man willing to dance with her. A sharp sting of vindictiveness rose within Aurelia.

Serves her right! she thought. Then her conscience pricked her, and she remembered the secret rhyme her mother had taught her.

Cupping a hand to her mouth so the other guests would not think her mad, she bowed her head and whispered the words of the hidden poem:

> *Toward others, always seek goodwill,*
> *Even if they've done you ill;*
> *All life's trials you may outlive,*
> *If only you learn to forgive.*

Though it pained her to wish her stepsister well, and though she had to wrestle with the anger surging in her heart, Aurelia obeyed her mother's command and whispered inwardly: *Lysandra, I forgive you. May you find the right path, and may you find love.*

All three looked up in astonishment at Aurelia's spangled white dress woven entirely in the pattern of the Ingridelite Weave. None of them recognized her. One by one, other heads turned as well, until the entire court was marveling at the most beautiful, bejeweled woman in the land.

The duke's son, Lord Samuel Chilvers, immediately approached her, the crowd of attendees parting for him. Aurelia extended her right hand, curled her index and middle fingers, pressed them to her left breast, and curtseyed.

Lord Samuel smiled, impressed.

"The pattern of your beautiful dress. Is that...that..." he began, but could not finish.

She nodded. "Yes, my liege. It is the Ingridelite Weave."

"Everything is in everything," he said, almost in a daze.

Aurelia took note of how he was becoming lost in the intricate, eternally moving threads in the dress. She understood their allure, for she had fallen under it herself.

"Careful staring too long at the weave, my liege," she said. "You lose yourself in the patterns. Please, distract your mind and ask me to dance."

"With pleasure," he replied, and offered his hand. "What is your name?"

"I cannot speak my name to, nor allow my name to be discovered by, any man while it is night."

"Very well, then. I will dance with you until the morning."

That night, Lord Samuel took her by the hand and danced with her, and no one else, and he never left her hand, but when anyone else came to ask her to dance, he said, "This lady is dancing with me."

Thus, they danced till a late hour of the night; and then she wanted to go home, and the duke's son said, "I shall go and take care of you to your home," for he wanted to see where the beautiful maiden lived.

Aurelia, however, knew this was too great a risk. If he followed her and learned her name from her father or step-relatives before sunrise, everything would be undone. Her gown would dissolve, and the duke's son would discover she was nothing more than a lowly servant in her father's house. And why would a man of Lord Samuel's stature want anything to do with a wretch like her?

After promising to see him at the festival the next day, Aurelia slipped away unawares and hurried toward the waiting stagecoach. Lord Samuel pursued her on horseback, but when she commanded the coachman to drive as fast as the dead could possibly fly, she vanished from his sight.

Chapter 4

The next day, when the final night of the feast would be held, and Aurelia's father and step-relatives were away from the house, Princess Kipira crawled over to Aurelia and wove a finer dress than the one she had worn the day before. This time, the stagecoach was larger and more elaborate, and instead of horses, it was drawn by animated lion-shaped webs.

When she arrived at the festival, every guest marveled at her beauty. The duke's son, however, had been waiting eagerly for her all evening, refusing every invitation from others, much to his parents' dismay. The moment he caught sight of her, he hurried forward, his brightest smile lighting his face as he showered her with affection and asked her to dance.

Aurelia agreed, and together they moved gracefully until late into the night. Whenever someone else approached with a request, Lord Samuel replied, just as he had the night before, "This lady is with me." At last, Aurelia knew it was time to go, for if she lingered any longer, she would not reach home until sunrise, even if the web-spun lions could travel as swiftly as the dead.

"Please, let me accompany you home," pleaded Lord Samuel.

"I cannot allow that. You must not know my name while it is still nighttime. And if you find where I live before the sun rises, everything will be ruined."

"But how so? What do you mean?"

"I don't know how, so please don't ask, my liege. However, if you desire to find me, then whatever you do, please don't ask for my name. Here is what you must do instead: go from house to house and ask every maiden if they can finish the poem I will recite to you. It is one known only to me and my departed mother.

Therefore, you must not repeat the final line to anyone, not even your own mother and father. The only maiden who can finish it is I, and that is how you will know you've found me, my liege."

"Tell me then, my lady. I insist."

Aurelia whispered in his ear:

> *Toward others, always seek goodwill,*
> *Even if they've done you ill;*
> *All life's trials you may outlive,*
> *If only you learn to forgive.*

"Repeat the first three lines to every maiden in your kingdom. The only one who knows, and who can give you the fourth line, is me. That is how you'll know you've found me, my liege."

Their eyes met, longing mirrored in each gaze. Softly, she gave him the smallest of kisses, then departed. Once again, he followed on his horse, but her chariot flew as fast as the dead.

The next day, Lord Samuel went to his father and declared, "I will take as my wife the lady who can finish these lines."

Then he recited:

> *Toward others, always seek goodwill,*
> *Even if they've done you ill;*
> *All life's trials you may outlive...*

When Duke Andrew inquired further, Lord Samuel told him all that had transpired between him and the young woman, but he dared not reveal the last line.

It was then proclaimed throughout the region of Shechem that every young maiden must prepare to receive the duke's son in her home, so that each might attempt to answer his question.

As the duke's son and his entourage, which included the Lady's Maids, travelled from house to house, asking the young women to complete the rhyme, every maiden failed, each offering either clever or clumsy guesses.

Word soon spread through Shechem, and before Lord Samuel arrived at any household, the maidens had already prepared lists of possible fourth lines. Yet none could answer correctly.

Meanwhile, Julia and Lysandra had worked together to invent as many endings as they could, while Aurelia quietly continued with her chores.

"She doesn't even bother to try to guess that fourth line," Lysandra scoffed.

"That's because she knows no one would want a filthy servant girl anyway," Julia jeered.

The two of them laughed as Aurelia mopped the floors.

However, when Lord Samuel finally entered their house, Oswald presented his wife and stepdaughter, leaving Aurelia to her chores.

Lord Samuel recited the three lines and asked Lysandra for the final one. She read every answer she had written, but none matched.

Frustrated, Lysandra burst into tears and screams. One of the guards sternly ordered her to control herself in the presence of the sovereign. Terrified, Julia begged for mercy and commanded her daughter to be silent.

"Are there any other young women in your home?" Lord Samuel asked.

Oswald shook his head.

Lord Samuel raised an eyebrow. "Are you absolutely certain?"

"I live here too!" Aurelia stepped from the kitchen into the parlour. She was covered in dirt and soot, her clothes ragged and filthy. Lord Samuel looked at her in surprise and recognition.

Turning to Oswald, he said, "Why did you lie to the nobility, after all it has done to prosper your household?"

"She is only a servant girl," Oswald replied. "She never attended your festival. She was busy cleaning the property."

"But every young maiden was required to attend. You, of all people, would know that. Why did you disregard a sacred custom of the land?"

Oswald began to tremble with fear.

To Aurelia, Lord Samuel said, "My lady, can you complete—"

Her face lit with the warmest smile. "If only you learn to forgive."

Lord Samuel beamed with delight, though his eyes glistened with both anger and sorrow.

"How could they treat you this way? How could they do this to you? You are the woman I have searched for everywhere."

"I don't know what could make them act so cruelly," she answered. "I can only hope that if I truly possess purity of heart, then it keeps me from comprehending the depth of their depravity."

Lord Samuel rushed across the room to her. "Oh, my lady, you are the purest of all hearts, and that is what makes you the most beautiful woman in all of Ingridel! You will never be mistreated again, for I will take you as my bride—if you'll have me."

"I was such a fool," Aurelia said. "I feared you'd spurn me if you knew what a dirty, lowly—"

He pressed a finger to her lips. "You are a beautiful woman of nobility. These rags, this dust and soot are but a thin disguise! Now, let me ask again. Would you be taken as my bride?"

Throwing herself into his arms, she said, "I do! I will!"

"Then please, my lady, tell me your name."

"Aurelia."

"Very fitting. Yours is the finest name in all Ingridel!"

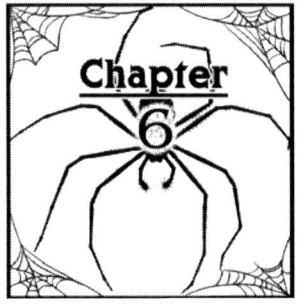

ord Samuel commanded his team to summon the Lady's Maids of the House of Chilvers, who had been waiting in their coach. Once they entered the house, they assisted Aurelia with bathing and grooming, preparing her as befits a Lady of the Court.

Meanwhile, he ordered Oswald to speak the absolute truth about all events since the death of his first wife, reminding him that to lie in the presence of a sovereign was punishable by beheading.

After a thorough interrogation, Lord Samuel declared, "A father who abandons his own daughter in this manner is unworthy to live. I sentence you and your entire household to the darkness of the dungeon, to spend the remainder of your days without food, water, or light. Each of you will die slowly, in an outer darkness as pitch black as your souls."

At this pronouncement, Aurelia, now fully adorned, entered the parlour. "Please, my lord! I beg of you, please do not carry out such a judgment against them."

"But...why?"

"Remember what my mother taught me on her deathbed."

Then she recited the first three lines:

Toward others, always seek goodwill,
Even if they've done you ill;
All life's trials you may outlive...

Then, Lord Samuel spoke the last line with Aurelia: "If only you learn to forgive."

She continued, "If we do not exercise mercy, then everything is in vain. All I have suffered was for naught. Every grievance I endured and forgave was to honour my mother. Punish them if you must, but please, temper your judgment with compassion."

Lord Samuel looked to Oswald and his adopted family. "None of you understood what a jewel you had in your midst. The very one you despised and abused has moved the heart of a sovereign, *my* heart, to compassion.

"I believe in justice, but I also believe in mercy. Instead of confinement in the dungeons, all three of you will be exiled. You will never again set foot on Ingridel's soil. You will be sent to Mahana to live out your days, and if any of you ever return, I promise you I will carry out my original sentence. I will hunt you down and have you executed.

"As for the wealth of your enterprise, because you have transgressed against the Crown, the House of Chilvers will absorb it all. You will be sent away with only a portion to rebuild in Mahana. Everything in this house now belongs to the Crown. You will leave in the clothes you are wearing, but you will keep your lives. Think wisely, look within, and strive to live out your remaining days with honour."

He then commanded his servants to prepare provisions, a horse-drawn coach, and a sum of money to send Oswald, Julia, and Lysandra safely away.

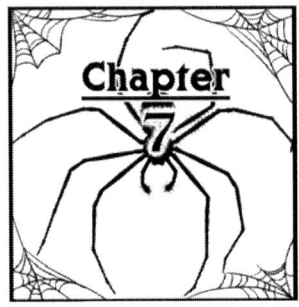

Princess Kipira had vanished on the second night of the festival, leaving Aurelia to wonder what had become of her. A month later, amid great pomp, Aurelia was married to Lord Samuel Chilvers.

After the ceremony, they entered a royal chariot prepared to take them to a remote cottage by a lake, all owned by Duke Andrew.

The estate, called A Fountain of Gardens, was reserved specifically for honeymoons. This place of romantic seclusion, picturesquely adorned with willow trees, flower gardens, and a tranquil lake, was named so because such a name carried the idea that from this private paradise, a fountain of new families could grow. It was the custom of Ingridelite royalty to consummate their marriages once they arrived at the chalet and no sooner.

As the chariot rattled over the cobblestone road, the canopying trees above casting shadows in the moonlight, Aurelia and Samuel held each other close.

Something drifting on the nighttime breeze outside the open window caught their eyes.

A long, unfurled scroll with writing upon it, undulating in the air. As it drew nearer, Aurelia realized it was woven entirely of webs.

Breaking free from her husband's embrace and trembling with the need to be in his arms again, she reached for the scroll as it floated through the window.

"A message! From Princess Kipira," she said.

"My dear, do you truly know the princess? Is she still alive? Are the wild rumours true?"

Reaching for the scroll as it floated through the window, Aurelia replied, "Yes, my lord. She is alive and well, though trapped in spider form, just as the rumours say. She cannot enter a village or city. She cannot enter any land owned by the Crown. Yes, it was she who helped me reach the festival. She wove my dress and my chariot."

"Many in our kingdom have tried and failed at the Ingridelite Weave," said Lord Samuel. "To our knowledge she was the only one living who could make it. And I thought it was you who had made your dress."

"I? Create a work of beauty such as that?"

"You are a work of beauty, darling," Lord Samuel said. "And we truly live in a world of wonders."

"Perhaps even worlds of wonders," Aurelia answered.

Briefly, her eyes searched beyond the cobblestones in the forest's shadows for any trace of Princess Kipira, yet she knew she would not find her anywhere.

Settling into her husband's embrace, she gently deflected his eager kisses, laughing softly as they teased one another.

At last, with a smile lingering on her lips, she turned her attention to the words Kipira had woven into the silken scroll.

Part Two
Metamorphosis

"Live on indeed, wicked one, but still hang; and let the same decree of punishment be pronounced against thy race, and against thy latest posterity, that thou mayst not be free from care in time to come."

—From Ovid's *Metamorphoses*, Book VI, Fable I
(Translated by Henry T. Riley)

earest Aurelia,

On the night we met by your mother's grave, I promised to explain why I did all this for you. As I am a woman of my word, I now send you this letter of explanation.

First, I must tell you how I, Princess Kipira, grew vainglorious of my ingenuity as a weaver, and how I challenged a peasant woman to a contest of skill in our shared art. She accepted, and when I saw myself outdone by one so lowborn, my pride turned to fury. I charged her with insolence and had her beheaded. With her final breath she cursed me, transforming me into a spider. Yet in her compassion, she left me a way to break her decree. By the end of this letter, your heart and mind will be prepared to understand my reasons for coming to your succour.

Once upon a time, when I was still in human form and you were just a little girl, everyone in Ingridel revered me not only as princess, but as a master weaver of wool. I knew—and still know—the secret of threading the Ingridelite Weave, and I designed intricately detailed tapestries depicting the history of our kingdom.

Indeed, my work continues to be celebrated throughout the land. You, of course, would know this, as any Ingridelite citizen does.

What few knew, however, was that behind my beauty and charm, behind my talent, I carried a heart of malice and pride.

It came to pass that word reached me of a poor peasant woman who could weave better than I. Winegrowers from across the country would leave their vineyards to behold her creations. Fishermen left their nets and docked their boats to do the same. They marveled at how she worked the wool with her fingers, and with the spindle and the needle. So graceful was her art that people said she "possessed a natural genius surpassing that of the great Princess Kipira." Whispers even spread that her tapestries came to life in the moonlight, so intricate, so full of detail were they.

I was so offended that one so lowborn could rival me that I summoned her to court and demanded she either cease weaving for the rest of her life or enter a contest of skill, in which the loser would forfeit her right to practice her craft.

I further explained that, as the daughter of Ingridel's ruling monarchs, I held the crown's authority; anyone who challenged my honour—or that of my family—was guilty of insolence, a form of treason, and by law, I possessed the right to punish offenders, even to the taking of a life.

I commanded my advisors to gather the finest weavers throughout the land and appoint them as judges, assuring them that their impartial decision would not be punished, even if it did not fall in my favour. Then my advisors set the rules: each of us was to weave our finest tapestry, telling any story we chose, and the one whose work not only told the best story but also surpassed the other in skill would be declared the winner. This was not merely a test of ability, but of imagination and creativity. The contest was scheduled to begin at sunrise and end at sundown.

The next morning, from dawn's rosy fingers caressing the rolling green hills around the capital to the silver threads of moonlight illuminating the land at dusk, we wove tirelessly, fervently, until the advisors called us to stop.

First, I told my story, using the panels of the tapestry I had woven as my illustrations.

Then the peasant woman, who had arranged her tapestries so the moonlight could bathe them, tapped a single thread. As the threads began to animate in the glow of the moon, she told her story. The entire court watched in awe.

At last, it was decided that she was the winner.

I was enraged! Unable to harm the judges, I, in my fury, declared the woman guilty of insolence.

I proclaimed that she must be beheaded that very night, and permitted her to speak her last words.

The woman said:

"Since you refuse to forfeit your right to practice your craft, you shall forfeit your form. You shall no longer weave as a human. Just as you take my life, I take your humanity. And from the moment my head falls from my neck, you will weave as a spider. You will be hated, feared, and alone, for many humans are repulsed by this race, and many creatures elude them. You will lose your beauty and appear as loathsome as your prideful, malicious heart.

"But unlike you, Princess Kipira, I possess compassion. So, I give you one way to escape your curse: you must perform an act of true kindness for someone. You must do a good deed with absolutely no thought of personal gain. It must be a purely selfless act, for that is the only form kindness takes.

"From this night forward, you will weave, and even all my great skill shall pass to you upon my death, yet you will remain despised as you despised me.

"Come not near any house of nobility in your spider form, or the curse shall hold you forever. I condemn you to forests and shadows, to weave beauty, yet to dwell in perpetual solitude.

"So, seek true kindness, Princess Kipira! Teach your spidery offspring to do the same, for should you perish before them, they may carry forward the chance to break the curse.

"Solve the mystery of kindness. Find this rare jewel of the heart, if you dare."

After she spoke those words, I spat in her face and laughed, then ordered one of my soldiers to execute her.

The instant her bloodied head thumped and rolled onto the floor, my own felt as if it were being crushed in a vice, my skull about to crack open like a walnut at a winter solstice festival and spill my brain. I screamed in agony, clawing at my temples.

My hands pressed against my head, but the pain would not subside. Sweat ran down my face. My body convulsed. My mind was a chaotic storm, threatening to tear me apart from the inside out.

"Please help me! It burns! Help me!"

No sooner had the words left my mouth than the peasant woman's severed head came to life, her face twisted into a snarl of rage, screaming, "I forbid you to help her! Lest I curse you too. Stay back! Flee from her!"

All my royal courtiers fled in terror.

Torment coursed through my entire body, as though I were being consumed by flames. Each wave was more intense than the last. Sweat matted my hair to my forehead, and my dress clung to me. In desperation, I tore and tore at my clothing. Fell to my hands and knees. Gasped for air.

Surrendering to the lowborn weaver's curse, I was both unmade and made in chrysalis—

Metamorphosis!

My body writhed and shifted,
Bones snapped and twisted,
Muscles tore, reforged—
Venomed fangs emerged.

My mouth, a bloody hollow,
Impossible to close or swallow.
From my forehead, black eyes grew;
My hands blackened, fingers fused.

A ticking, clicking litany
Replaced my screams of agony.
Dread filled my heart's dregs
As from my sides burst spider legs!

Then the peasant woman's head spoke again: "Run, Kipira! Leave this royal palace and its grounds. Never set foot upon the land of any duke or lord. Do not return until you are human again."

And mystically, driven by some powerful instinct, I fled on all eight legs, deep into the forest to dwell alone.

Now that you know my story, you can understand how I might hold the tenderest affection for you, how I truly love you as a sister, and yet still confess that everything I have done for you, Aurelia, was driven not by pure selflessness, but by my longing to regain my human form.

From completing your chores to weaving your dress and stagecoach, even to aiding your marriage to Lord Samuel, my actions were all touched by that hidden motive. Though your happiness brings me real joy, a mercenary thorn remains lodged in my heart, keeping me from showing true kindness to you...or to anyone at all.

My deeds awaken beneath the lesser light of hidden motives. Yet no matter how thoughtful they may appear, when brought into the greater light of truth, they are seen for what they are: hollow, empty. Works of selfishness. For a night they may seem noble, even kind, yet when the dawn of truth rises upon them, they dissolve into nothing, found wanting of lasting substance.

And therein lies my dilemma. How shall I escape the inherent selfishness that taints every action, even the noblest? I know that in me dwells no good thing. To will is present with me; but how to perform that which is good I find not. For the good that I would, I do not: but the evil which I would not, that I do. Oh wretch that I am! Who shall deliver me from the body of this death?

There is a sacred proverb: "You can catch the spider in your hand, yet it is found in royal palaces."

Permit me to share my interpretation. Perhaps the royal palaces symbolize our purest, most noble intentions toward others. And the spider, well, it is the emblem of our selfish nature. It spins its web for its own shelter and sustenance. It waits for the faintest tremor upon its threads, so that it may feed itself. Just as a spider is easily caught in the hand, so too may we easily perceive the motives that serve only ourselves. Yet that same cunning, creeping selfishness may dwell even within the grandest halls of our hearts—the royal palaces of our intentions—entangling all we do in its webs, and leaving us powerless, despite our best designs.

Still, there is hope that I may one day behold you again in my human form, as your sovereign princess, or perhaps even as your queen, should it take longer for me to uncover the mystery of kindness.

If anyone has taught me most of kindness, it is you, Aurelia. You are honest about the flaws of your spirit, yet you do not let them rule you.

There a strength greater than yourself that grants you power to be truly kind and to pass sentence upon your own selfishness. One day, I too may find that same source of strength, and when I do, I hope to drink deeply of its living waters.

I am now bound for the kingdom of Mahana, a stowaway upon the very coach that bears your exiled kin. Perhaps, as a stranger in a strange land, I may at last uncover the mystery of kindness.

Know always that you have won my friendship and my tenderest affections, dearest Aurelia.

Your Spider Sister,
Princess Kipira

<u>Part Three</u>
<u>A Fountain of Gardens</u>

"My beloved spake, and said unto me, Rise up, my love, my fair one, and come away. For, lo, the winter is past, the rain is over and gone; The flowers appear on the earth; the time of the singing of birds is come, and the voice of the turtle is heard in our land; The fig tree putteth forth her green figs, and the vines with the tender grape give a good smell. Arise, my love, my fair one, and come away."

—*Song of Solomon*, Chapter 2

"A fountain of gardens, a well of living waters, and streams from Lebanon. Awake, O north wind; and come, thou south; blow upon my garden, that the spices thereof may flow out. Let my beloved come into his garden, and eat his pleasant fruits."

—*Song of Solomon*, Chapter 4

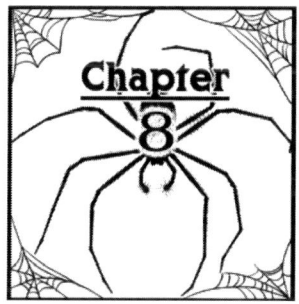

The two newlyweds had finished reading the letter, and both were in tears. They decided to sleep for the rest of their journey, lest their hearts be overcome with grief on their wedding night.

Finally, when the rosy-fingered dawn, enthroned in gold, began to show in heaven, the chariot entered A Fountain of Gardens. Both Lord Samuel and Lady Aurelia awakened.

"Her story is truly heartbreaking," he said. Before he could finish, sunlight streamed through the open window, striking the webbed scroll. It withered in their hands, unraveling into threads that crumbled to dust and vanished.

"All of Kipira's works, no matter how beautiful or finely woven, live only by moonlight," Aurelia said. "By morning, they dissolve into nothing."

The couple was escorted from the chariot while attendants carried their belongings into the chalet. In the meantime, Lord Samuel said, "Before we seal our vows, let us hold a moment of silence for Princess Kipira, our sovereign. And let us hope she finds a way to perform an act of true kindness, that she may be restored to us. If you are a praying woman, I ask you to lift her to God in your heart."

inally, they were alone, and the oak-framed canopy bed was their sheltering grove. Kissing the curve of her neck, Lord Samuel loosened the back of Lady Aurelia's dress, and it drifted to the floor. One hand rested at the small of her back while his lips returned to hers.

Meanwhile, her silken undergarments slid from her, and she kicked them aside.

"You're perfect," he whispered.

She smiled and sat at the foot of the bed, her golden hair spilling over her bare form. He shed his own garments, letting them fall in a pool around his feet, the belt buckle clinking against the floor.

Her eyes lingered on his. She was ravished with him, and she shivered beneath the heat of his gaze, which carried the full weight of his satisfaction in her. Hunger and yearning thrummed between them. They stood on the edge of a mystery, a mystery of their bodies and their covenant, waiting to unfold in splendour.

She drew him to her, and together they settled atop the bed.

She welcomed him, beckoned him, and he entered through her gate into the warmth of her garden, dewy with the fresh touch of rain. For a moment pain passed through her, and she trembled, a first bloom opening, until the feeling melted into—

a breath, a sigh, a rising cry

—sweet delight. The room filled with their eager words of passion, the rhythm of their bodies urging forth the delectation appointed for those married in love.

In the afterglow, skin pressed to skin, sweat mingled with sweat, they held each other beneath the gentle weight of the bedcovers. Kiss after kiss, they traced the curves of one another's smiles, resting in the quiet ecstasy of becoming one, the same.

From the Journal of Charlotte Sophia Janicker

The story of Aurelia, for all intents and purposes, is complete. Like so many heroines of our beloved wonder-tales, she has endured patiently at the hands of her tormentors, with a meekness befitting society's expectation of the fairer sex. Yet Providence, ever watchful, raised up for her a benevolent benefactor, through whose kindness she emerged from her trials and was rewarded with a union founded upon love, joined to a husband of noble birth.

Such a narrative is not singular, for the world has ever treasured stories of persecuted maidens who, by innocence, fortitude, and a touch of supernatural succour, are raised from abasement to honour—just as in the familiar tale of Cinderella, who is known throughout the world by many names: in China as Yeh-Shen, in Germany as Ashputtel, in Scotland as Rashin-Coatie, and so on. Time does not permit me to name them all.

In our present age, advocacy for women's rights is seldom voiced, and so these Cinderella narratives are fashioned from a philosophy that sympathizes with male tyranny, teaching that a woman's proper destiny lies in securing happiness through marriage to a wealthy, eligible bachelor.

Therefore, I find myself in a quandary regarding such tales; on the one hand, I despise the tyranny that shapes them, yet as an author and student of literature, I am compelled to turn their contrivances to the heroine's advantage.

The writers of these tales never seem to grasp the obvious, and I sought to correct this in my own telling. After such a wretched childhood, Cinderella deserves, at the very least, a joyful tumble in the hay with her handsome bridegroom, if only to set the drudgery of her past far behind her. In short, give that woman a whirlwind of bridal bliss. Heaven help the prudes who faint at the thought!

Nonetheless, I cannot help remembering the words of dear Mary Wollstonecraft, found in her *Vindication of the Rights of Woman*: "I do not wish them [women] to have power over men; but over themselves." She also observed, "Taught from their infancy, that beauty is woman's sceptre, the mind shapes itself to the body, and, roaming round its gilt cage, only seeks to adorn its prison." I do not deny that I delight in the sweetness and simplicity of the wonder tales of old; yet I hope that in writing one, I do not obscure a higher ideal from my readers' eyes: that one day a woman's worth may be measured not solely by her physical beauty, her meek endurance, or the husband she wins, but by the strength and enlargement of her own mind and spirit.

And may all women, like Scheherazade of old—described by Andrew Lang as having "the best masters in philosophy, medicine, history and the fine arts, and besides all this, her beauty excelled that of any girl"—possess the wit, courage, and perseverance to tell their own tales, define their own beauty, and secure for themselves both safety and honour.

—Charlotte Sophia Janicker
Victoria, Vancouver Island
the 24th of September, 1871

Appendix

Source Texts

Included here are the narratives that informed and inspired *Moonlight Desires*:

a — The Brothers Grimm version of *Cinderella*, which is entitled *Ashputtel* (meaning "The Little Ash Girl"), and
b — The story of *Arachne* from Ovid's *Metamorphoses*.

The reader is also encouraged to consult *Cinderella: The Ultimate Collection* (*Illustrated. Annotated. 29 Different Versions + Exclusive Bonus Features*), published by Enhanced Books, and which, at the time of this writing, is available on Amazon.

Ashputtel
by Jacob Grimm and Wilhelm Grimm

The wife of a rich man fell sick; and when she felt that her end drew nigh, she called her only daughter to her bed-side, and said, 'Always be a good girl, and I will look down from heaven and watch over you.' Soon afterwards she shut her eyes and died, and was buried in the garden; and the little girl went every day to her grave and wept, and was always good and kind to all about her. And the snow fell and spread a beautiful white covering over the grave; but by the time the spring came, and the sun had melted it away again, her father had married another wife. This new wife had two daughters of her own, that she brought home with her; they were fair in face but foul at heart, and it was now a sorry time for the poor little girl. 'What does the good-for-nothing want in the parlour?' said they; 'they who would eat bread should first earn it; away with the kitchen-maid!' Then they took away her fine clothes, and gave her an old grey frock to put on, and laughed at her, and turned her into the kitchen.

There she was forced to do hard work; to rise early before daylight, to bring the water, to make the fire, to cook and to wash. Besides that, the sisters plagued her in all sorts of ways, and laughed at her. In the evening when she was tired, she had no bed to lie down on, but was made to lie by the hearth among the ashes; and as this, of course, made her always dusty and dirty, they called her Ashputtel.

It happened once that the father was going to the fair, and asked his wife's daughters what he should bring them. 'Fine clothes,' said the first; 'Pearls and diamonds,' cried the second. 'Now, child,' said he to his own daughter, 'what will you have?' 'The first twig, dear father, that brushes against your hat when you turn your face to come homewards,' said she. Then he bought for the first two the fine clothes and pearls and diamonds they had asked for: and on his way home, as he rode through a green copse, a hazel twig brushed against him, and almost pushed off his hat: so he broke it off and brought it away; and when he got home he gave it to his daughter. Then she took it, and went to her mother's grave and planted it there; and cried so much that it was watered with her tears; and there it grew and became a fine tree. Three times every day she went to it and cried; and soon a little bird came and built its nest upon the tree, and talked with her, and watched over her, and brought her whatever she wished for.

Now it happened that the king of that land held a feast, which was to last three days; and out of those who came to it his son was to choose a bride for himself. Ashputtel's two sisters were asked to come; so they called her up, and said, 'Now, comb our hair, brush our shoes, and tie our sashes for us, for we are going to dance at the king's feast.' Then she did as she was told; but when all was done she could not help crying, for she thought to herself, she should so have liked to have gone with them to the ball; and at last she begged her mother very hard to let her go. 'You, Ashputtel!' said she; 'you who have nothing to wear, no clothes at all, and who cannot even dance—you want to go to the ball? And when she kept on begging, she said at last, to get rid of her, 'I will throw this dishful of peas into the ash-heap, and if in two hours' time you have picked them all out, you shall go to the feast too.'

Then she threw the peas down among the ashes, but the little maiden ran out at the back door into the garden, and cried out:

> *'Hither, hither, through the sky,*
> *Turtle-doves and linnets, fly!*
> *Blackbird, thrush, and chaffinch gay,*
> *Hither, hither, haste away!*
> *One and all come help me, quick!*
> *Haste ye, haste ye!—pick, pick, pick!'*

Then first came two white doves, flying in at the kitchen window; next came two turtle-doves; and after them came all the little birds under heaven, chirping and fluttering in: and they flew down into the ashes. And the little doves stooped their heads down and set to work, pick, pick, pick; and then the others began to pick, pick, pick: and among them all they soon picked out all the good grain, and put it into a dish but left the ashes. Long before the end of the hour the work was quite done, and all flew out again at the windows.

Then Ashputtel brought the dish to her mother, overjoyed at the thought that now she should go to the ball. But the mother said, 'No, no! you slut, you have no clothes, and cannot dance; you shall not go.' And when Ashputtel begged very hard to go, she said, 'If you can in one hour's time pick two of those dishes of peas out of the ashes, you shall go too.' And thus she thought she should at least get rid of her. So she shook two dishes of peas into the ashes.

But the little maiden went out into the garden at the back of the house, and cried out as before:

> *'Hither, hither, through the sky,*
> *Turtle-doves and linnets, fly!*
> *Blackbird, thrush, and chaffinch gay,*
> *Hither, hither, haste away!*
> *One and all come help me, quick!*
> *Haste ye, haste ye!—pick, pick, pick!'*

Then first came two white doves in at the kitchen window; next came two turtle-doves; and after them came all the little birds under heaven, chirping and hopping about. And they flew down into the ashes; and the little doves put their heads down and set to work, pick, pick, pick; and then the others began pick, pick, pick; and they put all the good grain into the dishes, and left all the ashes. Before half an hour's time all was done, and out they flew again. And then Ashputtel took the dishes to her mother, rejoicing to think that she should now go to the ball. But her mother said, 'It is all of no use, you cannot go; you have no clothes, and cannot dance, and you would only put us to shame': and off she went with her two daughters to the ball.

Now when all were gone, and nobody left at home, Ashputtel went sorrowfully and sat down under the hazel-tree, and cried out:

> 'Shake, shake, hazel-tree,
> Gold and silver over me!'

Then her friend the bird flew out of the tree, and brought a gold and silver dress for her, and slippers of spangled silk; and she put them on, and followed her sisters to the feast. But they did not know her, and thought it must be some strange princess, she looked so fine and beautiful in her rich clothes; and they never once thought of Ashputtel, taking it for granted that she was safe at home in the dirt.

The king's son soon came up to her, and took her by the hand and danced with her, and no one else: and he never left her hand; but when anyone else came to ask her to dance, he said, 'This lady is dancing with me.'

Thus they danced till a late hour of the night; and then she wanted to go home: and the king's son said, 'I shall go and take care of you to your home'; for he wanted to see where the beautiful maiden lived. But she slipped away from him, unawares, and ran off towards home; and as the prince followed her, she jumped up into the pigeon-house and shut the door. Then he waited till her father came home, and told him that the unknown maiden, who had been at the feast, had hid herself in the pigeon-house. But when they had broken open the door they found no one within; and as they came back into the house, Ashputtel was lying, as she always did, in her dirty frock by the ashes, and her dim little lamp was burning in the chimney. For she had run as quickly as she could through the pigeon-house and on to the hazel-tree, and had there taken off her beautiful clothes, and put them beneath the tree, that the bird might carry them away, and had lain down again amid the ashes in her little grey frock.

The next day when the feast was again held, and her father, mother, and sisters were gone, Ashputtel went to the hazel-tree, and said:

'Shake, shake, hazel-tree,

Gold and silver over me!'

And the bird came and brought a still finer dress than the one she had worn the day before. And when she came in it to the ball, everyone wondered at her beauty: but the king's son, who was waiting for her, took her by the hand, and danced with her; and when anyone asked her to dance, he said as before, 'This lady is dancing with me.'

When night came she wanted to go home; and the king's son followed here as before, that he might see into what house she went: but she sprang away from him all at once into the garden behind her father's house. In this garden stood a fine large pear-tree full of ripe fruit; and Ashputtel, not knowing where to hide herself, jumped up into it without being seen. Then the king's son lost sight of her, and could not find out where she was gone, but waited till her father came home, and said to him, 'The unknown lady who danced with me has slipped away, and I think she must have sprung into the pear-tree.' The father thought to himself, 'Can it be Ashputtel?' So he had an axe brought; and they cut down the tree, but found no one upon it. And when they came back into the kitchen, there lay Ashputtel among the ashes; for she had slipped down on the other side of the tree, and carried her beautiful clothes back to the bird at the hazel-tree, and then put on her little grey frock.

The third day, when her father and mother and sisters were gone, she went again into the garden, and said:

> *'Shake, shake, hazel-tree,*
> *Gold and silver over me!'*

Then her kind friend the bird brought a dress still finer than the former one, and slippers which were all of gold: so that when she came to the feast no one knew what to say, for wonder at her beauty: and the king's son danced with nobody but her; and when anyone else asked her to dance, he said, 'This lady is my partner, sir.'

When night came she wanted to go home; and the king's son would go with her, and said to himself, 'I will not lose her this time'; but, however, she again slipped away from him, though in such a hurry that she dropped her left golden slipper upon the stairs.

The prince took the shoe, and went the next day to the king his father, and said, 'I will take for my wife the lady that this golden slipper fits.' Then both the sisters were overjoyed to hear it; for they had beautiful feet, and had no doubt that they could wear the golden slipper. The eldest went first into the room where the slipper was, and wanted to try it on, and the mother stood by. But her great toe could not go into it, and the shoe was altogether much too small for her. Then the mother gave her a knife, and said, 'Never mind, cut it off; when you are queen you will not care about toes; you will not want to walk.' So the silly girl cut off her great toe, and thus squeezed on the shoe, and went to the king's son. Then he took her for his bride, and set her beside him on his horse, and rode away with her homewards.

But on their way home they had to pass by the hazel-tree that Ashputtel had planted; and on the branch sat a little dove singing:

'Back again! back again! look to the shoe!
The shoe is too small, and not made for you!
Prince! prince! look again for thy bride,
For she's not the true one that sits by thy side.'

Then the prince got down and looked at her foot; and he saw, by the blood that streamed from it, what a trick she had played him. So he turned his horse round, and brought the false bride back to her home, and said, 'This is not the right bride; let the other sister try and put on the slipper.' Then she went into the room and got her foot into the shoe, all but the heel, which was too large. But her mother squeezed it in till the blood came, and took her to the king's son: and he set her as his bride by his side on his horse, and rode away with her.

But when they came to the hazel-tree the little dove sat there still, and sang:

'Back again! back again! look to the shoe!
The shoe is too small, and not made for you!
Prince! prince! look again for thy bride,
For she's not the true one that sits by thy side.'

Then he looked down, and saw that the blood streamed so much from the shoe, that her white stockings were quite red. So he turned his horse and brought her also back again. 'This is not the true bride,' said he to the father; 'have you no other daughters?' 'No,' said he; 'there is only a little dirty Ashputtel here, the child of my first wife; I am sure she cannot be the bride.' The prince told him to send her. But the mother said, 'No, no, she is much too dirty; she will not dare to show herself.' However, the prince would have her come; and she first washed her face and hands, and then went in and curtsied to him, and he reached her the golden slipper. Then she took her clumsy shoe off her left foot, and put on the golden slipper; and it fitted her as if it had been made for her. And when he drew near and looked at her face he knew her, and said, 'This is the right bride.' But the mother and both the sisters were frightened, and turned pale with anger as he took Ashputtel on his horse, and rode away with her. And when they came to the hazel-tree, the white dove sang:

'Home! home! look at the shoe!
Princess! the shoe was made for you!
Prince! prince! take home thy bride,
For she is the true one that sits by thy side!'

And when the dove had done its song, it came flying, and perched upon her right shoulder, and so went home with her.

The Story of Arachne

From Ovid's *Metamorphoses*, Book VI, Fable I
(Translated by Henry T. Riley)

*A*rachne, vain-glorious of her ingenuity, challenges Minerva to a contest of skill in her art. The Goddess accepts the challenge, and, being enraged to see herself outdone, strikes her rival with her shuttle; upon which, Arachne, in her distress, hangs herself. Minerva, touched with compassion, transforms her into a spider.

Tritonia had meanwhile lent an ear to such recitals as these, and she approved of the songs of the Aonian maids, and their just resentment. Then thus she says to herself: "To commend is but a trifling matter; let us, too, deserve commendation, and let us not permit our divine majesty to be slighted without due punishment." And then she turns her mind to the fate of the Mæonian Arachne; who, as she had heard, did not yield to her in the praises of the art of working in wool.

She was renowned not for the place of her birth, nor for the origin of her family, but for her skill alone. Idmon, of Colophon, her father, used to dye the soaking wool in Phocæan purple. Her mother was dead; but she, too, was of the lower rank, and of the same condition with her husband. Yet Arachne, by her skill, had acquired a memorable name throughout the cities of Lydia; although, born of a humble family, she used to live in the little town of Hypæpæ.

Often did the Nymphs desert the vineyards of their own Tymolus, that they might look at her admirable workmanship; often did the Nymphs of the river Pactolus forsake their streams. And not only did it give them pleasure to look at the garments when made, but even, too, while they were being made, so much grace was there in her working. Whether it was that she was rolling the rough wool into its first balls, or whether she was unravelling the work with her fingers, and was softening the fleeces worked over again with long drawings out, equalling the mists in their fineness; or whether she was moving the smooth round spindle with her nimble thumb, or was embroidering with the needle, you might perceive that she had been instructed by Pallas.

This, however, she used to deny; and, being displeased with a mistress so famed, she said, "Let her contend with me. There is nothing which, if conquered, I should refuse to endure."

Pallas personates an old woman; she both places false gray hair on her temples, and supports as well her infirm limbs by a staff. Then thus she begins to speak: "Old age has not everything which we should avoid; experience comes from lengthened years. Do not despise my advice; let the greatest fame for working wool be sought by thee among mortals. But yield to the Goddess, and, rash woman, ask pardon for thy speeches with suppliant voice. She will grant pardon at my entreaty."

The other beholds her with scowling eyes, and leaves the threads she has begun; and scarcely restraining her hand, and discovering her anger by her looks, with such words as these does she reply to the disguised Pallas: "Thou comest here bereft of thy understanding, and worn out with prolonged old age; and it is thy misfortune to have lived too long. If thou hast any daughter-in-law, if thou hast any daughter of thy own, let her listen to these remarks. I have sufficient knowledge for myself in myself, and do not imagine that thou hast availed anything by thy advice; my opinion is still the same. Why does not she come herself? why does she decline this contest?"

Then the Goddess says, "Lo! she is come;" and she casts aside the figure of an old woman, and shows herself as Pallas. The Nymphs and the Mygdonian matrons venerate the Goddess. The virgin alone is not daunted. But still she blushes, and a sudden flush marks her reluctant features, and again it vanishes; just as the sky is wont to become tinted with purple, when Aurora is first stirring, and after a short time to grow white from the influence of the Sun.

She persists in her determination, and, from a desire for a foolish victory, she rushes upon her own destruction. Nor, indeed, does the daughter of Jupiter decline it, or advise her any further, nor does she now put off the contest. There is no delay; they both take their stand in different places, and stretch out two webs on the loom with a fine warp. The web is tied around the beam; the sley separates the warp; the woof is inserted in the middle with sharp shuttles, which the fingers hurry along, and being drawn within the warp, the teeth notched in the moving sley strike it. Both hasten on, and girding up their garments to their breasts, they move their skilful arms, their eagerness beguiling their fatigue.

There both the purple is being woven, which is subjected to the Tyrian brazen vessel, and fine shades of minute difference; just as the rainbow, with its mighty arch, is wont to tint a long tract of the sky by means of the rays reflected by the shower: in which, though a thousand different colors are shining, yet the very transition eludes the eyes that look upon it; to such a degree is that which is adjacent the same; and yet the extremes are different. There, too, the pliant gold is mixed with the threads, and ancient subjects are represented on the webs.

Pallas embroiders the rock of Mars in Athens, the citadel of Cecrops, and the old dispute about the name of the country. Twice six celestial Gods are sitting on lofty seats in august state, with Jupiter in the midst. His own proper likeness distinguishes each of the Gods. The form of Jupiter is that of a monarch. She makes the God of the sea to be standing there, and to be striking the rugged rocks with his long trident, and a wild horse to be springing forth out of the midst of the opening of the rock; by which pledge of his favor he lays claim to the city.

But to herself she gives the shield, she gives the lance with its sharp point; she gives the helmet to her head, and her breast is protected by the Ægis. She there represents, too, the earth struck by her spear, producing a shoot of pale olive with its berries, and the Gods admiring it. Victory is the end of her work. But that the rival of her fame may learn from precedents what reward to expect for an attempt so mad, she adds, in four different parts, four contests bright in their coloring, and distinguished by diminutive figures.

One corner contains Thracian Rhodope and Hæmus, now cold mountains, formerly human bodies, who assumed to themselves the names of the supreme Gods. Another part contains the wretched fate of the Pygmæan matron. Her, overcome in a contest, Juno commanded to be a crane, and to wage war against her own people. She depicts, too, Antigone, who once dared to contend with the wife of the great Jupiter; and whom the royal Juno changed into a bird; nor did Ilion protect her, or her father Laomedon, from assuming wings, and as a white crane, from commending herself with her chattering beak.

The only corner that remains, represents the bereft Cinyras; and he, embracing the steps of a temple, once the limbs of his own daughters, and lying upon the stone, appears to be weeping. She surrounds the exterior borders with peaceful olive. That is the close; and with her own tree she puts an end to the work.

The Mæonian Nymph delineates Europa, deceived by the form of the bull; and you would think it a real bull, and real sea. She herself seems to be looking upon the land which she has left, and to be crying out to her companions, and to be in dread of the touch of the dashing waters, and to be drawing up her timid feet.

She drew also Asterie, seized by the struggling eagle; and made Leda, reclining beneath the wings of the swan. She added, how Jupiter, concealed under the form of a Satyr, impregnated Antiope, the beauteous daughter of Nycteus, with a twin offspring; how he was Amphitryon, when he beguiled thee, Tirynthian dame; how, turned to gold, he deceived Danaë; how, changed into fire, the daughter of Asopus;

how, as a shepherd, Mnemosyne; and as a speckled serpent, Deois.

She depicted thee too, Neptune, changed into a fierce bull, with the virgin daughter of Æolus. Thou, seeming to be Enipeus, didst beget the Aloïdæ; as a ram, thou didst delude Theophane, the daughter of Bisaltis. Thee too the most bounteous mother of corn, with her yellow hair, experienced as a steed; thee, the mother of the winged horse, with her snaky locks, received as a bird; Melantho, as a dolphin. To all these did she give their own likeness, and the real appearance of the various localities.

There was Phœbus, under the form of a rustic; and how, besides, he was wearing the wings of a hawk at one time, at another the skin of a lion; how, too, as a shepherd, he deceived Isse, the daughter of Macareus. How Liber deceived Erigone, in a fictitious bunch of grapes; and how Saturn begot the two-formed Chiron, in the form of a horse. The extreme part of the web, being enclosed in a fine border, had flowers interwoven with the twining ivy.

Pallas could not blame that work, nor could Envy censure it. The yellow-haired Virgin grieved at her success, and tore the web embroidered with the criminal acts of the Gods of heaven. And as she was holding her shuttle made of boxwood from Mount Cytorus, three or four times did she strike the forehead of Arachne, the daughter of Idmon.

The unhappy creature could not endure it; and being of a high spirit, she tied up her throat in a halter. Pallas, taking compassion, bore her up as she hung; and thus she said: "Live on indeed, wicked one, but still hang; and let the same decree of punishment be pronounced against thy race, and against thy latest posterity, that thou mayst not be free from care in time to come."

After that, as she departed, she sprinkled her with the juices of an Hecatean herb; and immediately her hair, touched by the noxious drug, fell off, and together with it her nose and ears. The head of herself, now small as well throughout her whole body, becomes very small. Her slender fingers cleave to her sides as legs; her belly takes possession of the rest of her; but out of this she gives forth a thread; and as a spider, she works at her web as formerly.

A Note to Readers

Your Honest Reviews Matter!
Your feedback helps. If you have a moment,
please leave an honest review of this book on
Amazon and **Goodreads**.

Reviews guide other readers and give authors
valuable insight to keep improving their work.
Whether just a few words or a more detailed
reflection, your perspective is greatly
appreciated.

About the Author

David Tocher (pronounced "*talker*") is an award-winning, critically-acclaimed horror author. In 2025, he received the Literary Titan Gold Book Award in the category of Fiction for his novel *Spider Seeds*. He resides in the Okanagan region of British Columbia, Canada. His work has appeared in numerous fiction and non-fiction anthologies alongside renowned authors such as Kelley Armstrong, Tanith Lee, Graham Masterton, Ray Garton, Stephen Spignesi, Robin Furth, Bev Vincent, and many more.

In 2023, Next Chapter published *Letters from a Dead World*, Tocher's collection of short stories with an introduction by Nancy Kilpatrick. In 2019, Tocher's anthology *Canadian Dreadful* garnered high praise from David Morrell, the esteemed author of *First Blood*. Morrell described it as a "harrowing tour of the northern landscape that will leave you both dazzled and terrified." Tocher's personal essay entitled *I'm Gonna Scare the Hell Out of You...And That's a Promise* is featured in *Stephen King Dollar Baby: The Book* by Anthony Northrup. Furthermore, Tocher's opinion essay, *He is the Doorway: Stephen King's Fiction as a Gateway to Classic Literature*, can be found in Northrup's *Stephen King Dollar Baby: The Sequel*.

Tocher is an Associate Producer for several motion pictures, including the 2023 remake of *Spider Baby*, or *The Maddest Story Ever Told*, starring horror icons Ron Chaney and Brinke Stevens; Dawn Fields' acclaimed anthology of short films entitled *The Edge of Her Mind*, showcasing the talents of women filmmakers and featuring the renowned Lance Henriksen from *Aliens* and *Near Dark*; and B*eyond the Gates of Hell*, also starring Brinke Stevens. When he's not writing or exploring literary classics, he enjoys the unique charm of B-movie horror films and watching a good baseball game.

Visit **www.DavidTocher.com** to learn more.

SCAN ME!

Subscribe to My Newsletter

You've reached the end of the story...but some doors are meant to stay open.

Subscribe to my newsletter to get first access to upcoming releases, exclusive content, early sneak peeks, behind-the-scenes lore, and curious surprises from my writing desk.

OTHER BOOKS FROM
JaFra Publishing

The Legacy of Frankenstein by Franklin E. Wales
Beyond Frankenstein by Jeffrey Kosh
Quoth the Raven Once More by Maynard Blackoak
Redline by Franklin E. Wales
It Ain't Fancy by Jacki WildmanWales

www.jafrapublishing.com

Manufactured by Amazon.ca
Acheson, AB

32933392R00067